MARC BROWN

Manners Matter

Arthur and his friends were
taking turns shooting baskets.

"You're up, Buster," said Francine.

"Watch me and weep," joked Buster.
"I can make this basket with my eyes closed."

"I want to shoot one," said Binky.

Binky stepped in front of him and grabbed the ball. He threw the ball into the basket. "Not bad, huh?" Binky bragged.

"Binky Barnes, that was totally rude!" said Muffy.

"It was Buster's turn," sniffed Prunella. "And I was after him."

"Some people just have no manners," said Francine.

"Who needs manners?" Binky said. "I get what I want without them."

Then Binky walked away, whistling.

"We can't just let him get away with that," said Francine.

"What can we do?" asked Buster.

"We could sign Binky up for a manners class," suggested Muffy.

"Can you see Binky in a manners class?" said Francine.

"Sure," Arthur laughed. "Please pass the tea, Master Binky."

"And don't forget to curl your pinky," added Buster.
"Hey, that rhymes!"

Everyone laughed.

"I think Muffy might be onto something," the Brain said.

"A manners class?" asked Francine.

"No. Manners lessons," said the Brain. "Binky needs to learn the importance of being polite."

"How?" asked Buster.

"We could be rude to him all day so he sees what it feels like," said Arthur.

"I like it," nodded Francine.

"Being rude won't be easy for me," said Muffy. "But I'll try."

"This will be an interesting behavior study," said the Brain.

"I hope it works!" said Buster.

Later, Arthur and Buster saw Binky downtown watching a street performer.

Arthur and Buster pushed their way in front of Binky. Then Buster put on his cowboy hat.

"Hey!" said Binky. "I can't see!"

"Guess you'd better move then," said Buster.

"I was here first," insisted Binky.

"Wow!" said Buster. "That guy just ate fire!"

"Incredible," said Arthur.

"I missed it," Binky grumbled. "Move, or I'm going to..."

"You're going to what?" asked Mr. Ratburn, Binky's teacher.

"Nothing, Mr. Ratburn, sir," Binky sputtered.
"I didn't see you there."

"I was having a nice time until you guys came along,"
said Binky. Then he stomped away.

Around the corner, Binky ran into Muffy and Francine.
They were fixing Francine's bike.

"Where's that bike pump?" asked Francine.

Binky saw the pump on the ground. He handed it to Francine.

Francine grabbed the pump from Binky and blew up her tire. "Okay, Muffy. All set," said Francine.

"Isn't there something you want to say to me?" asked Binky.

"Yeah," answered Muffy. "Move."

Then she and Francine rode away.

Binky stared at them in shock. "You do something nice for somebody, and what do you get?"

Just then, the Brain whizzed by—right through a puddle.

Mud splattered all over Binky.

The Brain screeched to a halt. "How unfortunate," he said.

Binky waited for the Brain to apologize.

"Fascinating abstract pattern," said the Brain as he rode away.

"I don't believe this," muttered Binky. "Even the Brain..."

Binky headed home to change his clothes. On the way, he saw Prunella unloading groceries.

"Binky, hold this bag," said Prunella.

Too surprised to refuse, Binky took the bag.

Prunella closed the car door and grabbed the bag. She walked into her house without another word.

"Hasn't anyone ever heard of 'please' or 'thank you'?" said Binky.

Binky turned to go. A little boy on a scooter was blocking the sidewalk.

"Out of my way," said Binky. The little boy froze with fear.

Binky saw Prunella watching him.

"*Please*," he added loud enough for Prunella to hear.

The little boy smiled. He moved his scooter.

Binky smiled back.

"Thank you," Binky said.

The next day at the grocery store, Binky accidentally bumped into a lady. "Excuse me," he said.

The lady smiled. "It's such a pleasure to meet a polite young man like you," she said.

Binky blushed.

"Some kids today don't even know what manners are," the lady said.

Later, Arthur and his friends were on their way to the ice cream shop.

"Move it!" Binky shouted.

Francine groaned. Their plan wasn't working.

They turned the corner to see Binky glaring at a big bully.

"Get lost," said Binky. "And stop picking on little kids."

The bully ran. A small boy hid behind Binky.

"Thanks, Binky," he said.

"You're welcome," said Binky.

"Did I hear what I think I heard?" asked Francine.

"High five, Brain!" said Buster.

"We did it," said Muffy.

"What?" asked Binky.

"Oh, nothing," said Arthur. "Want to get some ice cream, Binky?"

Binky looked suspicious.

"You've all been acting pretty weird lately," he said.

"Really?" said Arthur.

At the ice cream shop, the Brain's mom handed Binky his cone.

"Thanks," said Binky.

Brain's mom did a double-take. "You're welcome, Binky," she said, adding another scoop to his cone.

"Wow!" said Binky, balancing his triple-dip cone. "This manners thing really works!"